Touched by the Seasons

To every thing there is a season, and a time to every purpose under the heaven:

A time to be born, and a time to die; a time to plant, and a time to pluck up that which is planted;

A time to kill, and a time to heal; a time to break down, and a time to build up;

A time to weep, and a time to laugh; a time to mourn, and a time to dance;

A time to cast away stones, and a time to gather stones together; a time to embrace, and a time to refrain from embracing:

A time to get, and a time to lose; a time to keep, and a time to cast away;

A time to rend, and a time to sew; a time to keep silence, and a time to speak;

A time to love, and a time to hate; a time of war, and a time of peace.

Ecclesiastes 3:1-8

ISBN 0-89542-056-2 395

SPRING

Spring sings out with the freshness of discovery. Newborn things awaken to life! This is the time people learn to appreciate and absorb the knowledge nature is sharing. Minds are stimulated, and creative boundaries burst. Imagination is explored and people enjoy a freedom of expression.

Jan F. Engel

Oh, the
Starlit Eyes
of Children

Oh, the starlit eyes of children
Are a compliment to heaven;
How those gleaming eyes can sparkle,
Be they three or be they seven!

You find mirth and joy and laughter
Mirrored in their radiant glow;
The delight that in them dances
Far outshines new-fallen snow.

All the rhapsodies of childhood
In that glitter are revealed;
All the merry pranks and secrets
For a moment lie concealed,

When some momentary sorrow
Strikes those eyes so innocent,
Tears betray no sign of lingering
Once the first impulse is spent.

They relate of great successes
Or a treasured, newfound friend,
Or reflect a glowing vision
Having fairies without end.

They will twinkle at the story
Of the cat who ate the mice,
But they'll really start to listen
If the tale is versa vice.

Whether stirred by joy or humor,
Whether filled with playful glee,
Children's eyes show carefree times
Which we've enshrined in memory.

Ed Brandt

A Child
Should Dwell

A child should dwell where there are fields
And woodlands to explore.
Where he can learn the names of trees
And study earth's sweet lore.

Where he can make a friend
Of every timid forest creature
And learn about all growing things,
With nature for his teacher.

A place where he can race the wind,
And feel the kiss of sun,
And walk barefooted in the grass,
Or wade in some cool run.

A little one should know a spot
To find the first shy flowers
That blossom in a hidden place
Caressed by April showers.

Oh, if a child can romp and play
In woods . . . find fields to trod . . .
He'll learn the secrets of the earth
And catch a glimpse of God!

Betty Stuart

The Tender Time

Now is the tender time
When waters are gentle mists,
When suns have warming fingers,
When earth is soft and damp,
And hearts are stirring full.

Now is the tender time
When trees wear thin green lace,
When tulips beg attention,
When puppies have wet noses,
And hearts are stirring full.

Now is the tender time
When pussy willow is smoke,
When new moons hang so close,
When birdsong fills the air,
And hearts are stirring full.

Now is the tender time
When earth is full of young,
When cries are soft with joy,
When love is new at being,
And hearts are stirring full.

Evelyn Julian Dallas

Home

My happy song shall echo from the walls, my cheerful smile shall keep it fair and bright; and warmth and welcome shall pervade the halls so all who dwell herein shall know delight, and call it home.

Maurine Hathaway

Happy is the family whose members play together and work together and know one another's hearts. They think differently, but their thoughts meet with understanding. They follow different ways, but their actions have a common purpose. The unities of such a family are like silken threads, strong and true, and woven together harmoniously.

Author Unknown

Friendship House

The sun is always shining in
The home where friendship lives,
Where life is measured not by tears
But by the joy it gives,
Where hands are clasped in greeting
And the warmth of love is shown,
And every word is spoken in
An understanding tone.

The flowers are forever fair
Where kindly thoughts abide,
Where there is never any room
For jealousy or pride,
Where sympathy and sacrifice
And cheerfulness prevail,
And smiles of true encouragement
Are like an endless trail.

The sun is always shining,
And the sky is always clear
Where friendship lives, and sentiments
Are honest and sincere.

James J. Metcalfe

Childhood on a Farm

Can you think of any nicer place
To raise a growing child
Than a farm with lots of trees and vines
And flowers growing wild,
And a shallow, pebble-bottomed creek
To cool his busy feet?
How could any home for any child
Be nearly as complete?

I was raised in such a setting
And remember vividly
Wild strawberries, mild Mayapples,
And our old black walnut tree,
Green gooseberries, round and sour,
That we picked to make a pie,
Sweet wild roses by the roadside
To enjoy as we walked by.

Sturdy vines that hung from branches,
Nature's swings for little folks,
Backyard forest full of maples,
Slippery elms and gnarled oaks,
And, of course, our private "river,"
Pebble-bottomed, clean and clear,
Where our mother did the washing
On the warm days of the year.

There we often splashed and waded,
Skipped flat rocks and sailed our boats,
Watching insects skim the water,
Hearing tree frogs trill their notes,
And at evening seeing fireflies
Flashing on and off at will,
Till the last gray light of daytime
Faded from behind the hill.

What could be more fascinating,
What more filled with joy and charm
Than the living of one's childhood
On so wonderful a farm?

Linnea Holmberg Bodman

Friendship

Casual friendships come and go much as the currents ebb and flow. The swells and ripples that they make leave mixed emotions in their wake. For some friends drift with changing tide. They come on strong and then subside, only to crash upon the shore, disappear and be seen no more!

Others are strong enough to stand the changing tides and shifting sand. And what sets these friendships apart? Affinity of mind and heart, love much more than just a token, thoughts understood yet unspoken, a common bond, a mutual goal, an understanding heart and soul, a hand outstretched in time of need, a thoughtful and a friendly deed.

These little things that mean so much are strokes of friendship's velvet touch!

Donita M. Dyer

Sharing

If I have beauty, I must share it
As I pass along.
If a melody I have,
I owe the world a song.
If I have laughter in my heart
And there is need to spare,
It is but right that laughter
With someone I should share.

If I can paint the beauty
Of a lovely flower,
And hold for the world to see
What fades within the hour;
If I have a happy thought
That with someone I share . . .
I have used the talent given
By Him who put it there.

Lucille McBroom Crumley

When Springtime Comes

Spring comes in on soft wings. Cool whisperings among the branches as buds open, spilling color and perfume on winey air. Secrets are shared in small places. A green fern, a graceful lily— both surprises from the good earth. A purple violet winks when its green leaf cover is gently laid aside. Birdsong fills the air as martins plan and spring clean in the birdhouse which towers over the greening lilac bushes. On the evening breeze at dusk, the whippoorwill's sad call seems endless. And man, wiping away the cobwebs of the long cold winter, views the greening earth and lays out seeds with love in the soft, moist earth. Warming sunshine and gentle rain all come to visit again in the springtime.

Ann Silva

Rediscovery

So long I had forgotten
The intricate pattern of a leaf,
The veined beauty of a rock,
The perfection of an acorn cup,
The comforting feel of moss,
The rugged strength of tree roots,
The delicate beauty of a wild flower.

So long I had forgotten
The soothing sound of wind through trees,
The complex simplicity of boughs and leaves
In skyward silhouette, on looking up;
And the languid passage of cloud ships
Over the sky's blue waters.
Oh, blessed peace!

I feel the quiet power of earth
Flowing into me,
Strength from rock and sky and tree.
Oh, blessed rediscovery!

Clara Lundie Crawford

The warmth of the sun
Embraces the soul
As springtime invades the earth;
Bright green leaves
And the return of grass,
Animals filled with mirth;
Cheerful birds
And frolicking horses;
Spring . . . the season of rebirth!

Bonnie R. Climo

Listen with Your Heart

Go out, go out I beg of you
   And taste the beauty of the wild.
   Behold the miracle of earth
   With all the wonder of a child.
Walk hand in hand with nature's god
   Where scarlet lilies brightly flame.
Make footprints in the virgin sod,
   By some clear lake without a name.

Listen not only with your ears,
   But make your heart a listening post.
Travel above the timberline,
   Make fires on some lonely coast,
Breathe the high air of snow-crowned peaks,
   Taste fog and kelp and salty tides,
Go pitch your tent amid the pines
   Where golden sun and peace abide.

Follow the trail of moose and deer,
   The wild goose on his lonely flight,
Savor the fragrance of the wild,
   The sweetness of a northern night.
Drink deep of distance, rest your eyes
   Where centuries of peace have lain,
And let your thoughts go winging out
   Beyond the realm of man's domain.

Lay hold upon the out-of-doors
   With heart and soul and seeking brain,
You'll find the answer to all life
   Held in the sun and wind and rain.
Where'er you walk by land or sea
   The page is clear for all who seek,
If you will listen with your heart
   And let the voice of nature speak.

Edna Jaques

Friends

See how he gallops, graceful and free,
Striding along so effortlessly.
See how he raises his head high and proud,
Challenging all in a voice clear and loud!
Yet when I whistle, he stops and turns
And comes to me with eyes that yearn
For a handout sweet and a bite to eat . . .
And the love shines out of those big dark eyes.
He's not really wild, he just likes to pretend.
He's my yearling colt and I'm his friend.

Pat Lembcke

The sea runs without end,
sometimes slowly, sometimes swiftly,
eternally creating
formations and images in the sand.
It is the same with life.
We live,
some of us quickly,
others with caution, taking time,
and the experiences
create lines and impressions,
and our faces,
like the sand,
show what happens in our souls.

Janice Blue

As long as I live, I'll hear waterfalls and birds and winds sing. I'll interpret the rocks, learn the language of flood, storm and avalanche. I'll acquaint myself with the glaciers and wild gardens, and get as near the heart of the world as I can.

John Muir

To live by the sea
is to hear the sound
of time and eternity,
to hear the soft whisper
of the water washing
the sand of the shore,
gently swaying
the moments of time
or to hear the hard slap
of the white cap
upon the rock, loudly
speaking the eons
of eternity . . .
this is to live
by the sea.

Arthur J. Weber

To see a world in a grain of sand,
And a heaven in a wild flower,
Hold infinity in the palm of your hand,
And eternity in an hour.

William Blake

Beauty is Silent

Silently, softly, the dusk settles down.
Slender fingers of a disappearing sun
grasp at the coverlet of night and tuck its
luxuriant warmth down around a sleeping
earth. And all the earth creatures are
hushed in this instant of peacefulness.

Slowly, subtly, the wild rose stretches its
smooth contours in the gentle breeze to
capture the half moon of silver which
appears without a sound. Small leaves are
sifted noiselessly from an old tree, the
sound of their fall muffled by unmoving
grasses. And all the plant things are
quieted in this moment of beauty.

Shifting shadows on the still surface of a
hidden pool lighten and darken with the
moods of a saffron sun which rests against
the pale cushion of sky. And all men are
mute in this moment of inspiration when
they look up to their Creator.

Peggy DeShields

Through the Afterglow

Love is not gone when it has ceased to flame.
The smoldering embers hold the hidden spark.
Although the kindling may not be the same,
The mind it lights will never sense the dark.

And two who come at last to autumn's sun,
Rejoicing through the twilight of the years,
Although they know that life's best work is done,
Will face the night with eyes too proud for tears.

Then only can the inner spirit know
Love's benediction through the afterglow.

May Smith White

from Song of the Open Road

Afoot and light-hearted I take to the open road,
Healthy, free, the world before me,
The long brown path before me leading wherever I choose.

Henceforth I ask not good-fortune, I myself am good-fortune,
Henceforth I whimper no more, postpone no more, need nothing,
Done with indoor complaints, libraries, querulous criticisms,
Strong and content I travel the open road.

The earth, that is sufficient,
I do not want the constellations any nearer,
I know they are very well where they are,
I know they suffice for those who belong to them.

The earth expanding right hand and left hand,
The picture alive, every part in its best light,
The music falling in where it is wanted, and stopping where it is
     not wanted,
The cheerful voice of the public road, the gay fresh sentiment of
     the road.

O highway I travel, do you say to me Do not leave me?
Do you say Venture not— if you leave me you are lost?
Do you say I am already prepared, I am well-beaten and undenied,
     adhere to me?

O public road, I say back I am not afraid to leave you, yet I love you,
You express me better than I can express myself,
You shall be more to me than my poem.

I think heroic deeds were all conceiv'd in the open air, and all
     free poems also,
I think I could stop here myself and do miracles,
I think whatever I shall meet on the road I shall like, and
     whoever beholds me shall like me,
I think whoever I see must be happy.

Walt Whitman

We travel along the road of life hardly knowing what we are, yet always daring to be something; seldom saying what we mean, but never afraid to have meaning; sometimes failing in our endeavors, though never tempted to cease trying: seeking satisfaction at every level, yet never defining happiness: often apologizing for our existence, while realizing that life is its own excuse.

But the real joy of our otherwise insignificant efforts is that we are never quite satisfied to be on the left, or right, or in the middle of that road.

We are always attempting to change its direction.

Alan Ashley Pitt

SUMMER

Summer fills people with a glow that warms their hearts. Things are felt intensely, and beauty and love is observed in all things. People open up and share themselves with the world. The heartbeat of the earth slows down, and days become long and fulfilled.

Jan F. Engel

A Definition of Time

Time is the winding tape of the universe. By it we measure space otherwise illimitable. It is also the fourth dimension. Beyond it lies the Infinite Wisdom that baffles understanding and the mysteries of eternity that man shall never know.

Time marches with the sun and the stars. Like the air, it comes to our service at birth for use during a brief and uncertain period. Unlike the air, it is never renewed. Nor can it be compressed or expanded.

Nothing is so inexorable. Time makes no concessions or compromises. How it may be employed, if employed at all, is a matter of the utmost indifference. Time utters no commands, offers no advice. Only the liveliest is sensitive to the suggestions of its silent passage. With the hours in their stately procession, we may proceed with a purpose to make the most of an opportunity that will never come again, or straggle aimlessly from cradle to grave.

Time is the mark of immortality; and man, in tragic folly, uses it as if a day or a year were but a trifle from an inexhaustible store. He views the brighter prospect of tomorrow while he wastes only today; and he never knows that the moment passing unused is a jewel falling into the sea of the infinite, and gone forever.

Orville R. Hagans

Camping

Music of fire . . . Freedom to think . . . The smell of burning pitch-pine wood . . . Smoke from the campfire . . . The expectation to explore . . . Letting the sun be my wristwatch . . . The gentle warmth of tender, early morning light . . . Conversation with new-made friends . . . A camera in my lap . . . Pleasure in my nap . . . The lines of the trees . . . Splendor of blue sky . . . An insect passing by . . . The joy of luxurious leisure . . . The distant clang of horseshoe stakes . . . The art of living in the present, but also thoughts of the remembered past . . . The quietude of heart at ease . . . Ashes in the breeze.

Larry Roger Clark

Between
the Clouds

Between the clouds the sky is blue,
A bit of heaven shining through. If a
gold edge gilds the grey, the sunshine
can't be far away.

Though the clouds look full of rain,
It is useless to complain. Do not let
your moods be swayed by the weather,
light and shade.

Fortune changes like the sky; spirits
drop and hopes soar high. Life is full
of ups and downs, failures, triumphs,
smiles and frowns.

Keep on looking for a sign, then some
day the sun will shine. Keep your
mental vision clear, and the blue skies
will appear.

Patience Strong

The rain has threaded grass with silver beads
And polished swiftly all the greening leaves,
And houses bleakly huddled in the wet
Have shining pendants dripping from the eaves.

No smallest patch of blue shows through the clouds
With hope of weather fair,
But rain unlocks the roses' lovely hearts
And perfumes all the air.

The birds and bees have gone to hive and nest
Until the warming sun shines forth again,
And children, too, must stay awhile indoors,
Have dreams beyond a glistening windowpane.

Elsie Pearson

Quiet Times

Quiet dew upon the grass
In an early morning hour
Transforms the commonplace
Into scenes of misty grandeur.

This crystal beauty cannot last,
Soon it will simply disappear;
But, in these quiet moments, it bestows
Sweet freshness on a day's beginning.

God provides the quiet times
And moments of great inspiration
To strengthen us for hours of stress
And give us time for meditation.

Martha Creekmore

The Grass

Gather a single blade of grass, and examine for a minute, quietly, its narrow sword-shaped strip of fluted green. Nothing, as it seems there, of notable goodness or beauty. A very little strength, and a very little tallness, and a few delicate long lines meeting in a point, not a perfect point, but blunt and unfinished, by no means a creditable or apparently much cared for example of Nature's workmanship; made, as it seems, only to be trodden on today, and tomorrow to be cast into the oven; and a little pale and hollow stalk, feeble and flaccid, leading down to the dull brown fibres of roots. And yet, think of it well, and judge whether of all the gorgeous flowers that beam in summer air, and of all strong and goodly trees, pleasant to the eyes and good for food, stately palm and pine, strong ash and oak, scented citron, burdened vine, there be any by man so deeply loved, by God so highly graced, as that narrow point of feeble green.

John Ruskin

More Than a Word

Summer is more than just a word— it is
A young man's freedom to explore the green
Part of his world: all hills and trees are his
To climb; the scent of pine is sharp and clean
To nostrils long confined to dusty book;
And eyes can roam the far horizon's rim
Or follow the silver threading of a brook . . .
Summer is more than just a word to him!

It is a song, a slow, daylong adventure
Of browsing through a meadow deep with hay,
Or suddenly running barefoot without censure,
To paddle in a stream along the way.

Summer is more than words— it's food and drink
To those who need to dream awhile . . . and think.

Lydia B. Atkinson

The Quiet Things

Life's sweetest things are often quiet things:
The hush before the morning bird first sings,
The peaceful stillness at the break of day,
A silent pool where dappled sunbeams play,
The light caress of wind, the gentle rain,
Sweet-scented dusk, the quiet after pain,
The silent wonder in the questing eyes
Of children seeing bits of paradise.
Stars hung like jewels in the far, still sky,
An arch of rainbow lights, a butterfly,
The fire glow of flickering quietude,
Quintessence of a hushed and golden mood.
Just quiet things . . . a tranquil, greening hill,
A stream serene, the nighttime, sweet and still,
Can fill the soul with deep content and peace
And from all ills the heart can find release.

Ruth B. Field

Seaside Thoughts

Friendship is like the rolling sea,
And each wave always brings
A thought of friends I cherish most
And my heart fairly sings.

The white tops riding far at sea
Remind me of those friends,
Where though the miles stretch far between,
Our friendship never ends.

And as the tide breaks on the shore
I watch it ebb and flow,
As memories of friends held dear
So fondly come and go.

Then as I look far out to sea
Where water meets the sky,
Just as Heaven and earth are joined,
So friendship, two hearts tie.

Vera Hardman

There is a pleasure in the pathless woods, there is a rapture
on the lonely shore, there is society, where none intrudes,
by the deep sea, and music in its roar: I love not man the
less, but nature more, from these our interviews, in which I
steal from all I may be, or have been before, to mingle
with the universe, and feel what I can ne'er express, yet
cannot all conceal.

Byron

To a Friend

Let the great out-of-doors embrace you . . . Let it take you in its arms . . . And caress you . . . With its cool breezes . . . And its warm sunlight . . . Let it thrill you with its beauty . . . And soothe you with its harmony . . . Let it open new doors to your soul . . . And lead new pathways to your heart . . . Let it weave its pattern upon your life . . . Let it sing to you . . . Then there could not be any real darkness anywhere . . . For even that will have its stars.

Lorice Fiani Mulhern

THE HELPING HAND
Emile Renouf

My Friend

My friend is more a treasure . . . Than the purest minted gold . . . Than all the wealth of riches . . . The worldly strive to heap and hold . . . For his friendship is my fortune . . . My happiness and prize . . . And his faithfulness much dearer . . . Than the treasures of men's eyes.

He heaps my heart with gladness . . . With things that gold can never buy . . . With boundless joy and rapture . . . Beneath the fairest sky . . . For the bond of love between us . . . Grows stronger all the while . . . As we match strides together . . . Up another winding mile.

My friend is my real fortune . . . And the treasure of my heart . . . My every dream and song . . . With all the blessings he imparts . . . And men may yearn for riches . . . And things of temporal worth . . . But I have found my treasure . . . And the greatest wealth on earth.

Joy Belle Burgess

The Season of the Soul

It is the time when all things are
Crisp and tart to the senses,
When peace comes as easy to the mind
As sleep to the newborn.

It is the time when rainbows
Are free to linger as they feel,
While the robin's notes, the sharps
And flats, echo off the rose's dew.

It is the time for wearing flowers
In your hair and nothing on your feet,
So you can feel the wind and the grass
And they can touch you in your sleep.

It is the time for dreams to come
While you are awake, that you
Might sing and dance and fly
As you knew you always could.

It is the time for speaking freely,
Unashamed and unhurt, understanding
You will be understood and knowing
You will comprehend it all.

It is the time for knowing others in a
Closer way than you ever thought you could
And learning that they are not that different,
That their hopes and fears are just like yours.

It is the time when you come to know yourself
And realize that you are more than you thought.
You are the whole, boundless and unfettered.
It is the time; it is the season of the soul.

Robert Hengfuss

Symphony of Summer

There's a symphony that greets the ears
As the summer sounds unfold,
From the whisper of wind in the pines
To the drums of thunder rolled.
All the birds trill their melodies sweet
And the streams echo the strains,
While the insects' call a cadence beat
Down the mountains to the plains.

There's a symphony that greets the eyes
As the summer colors blend,
Snow-white clouds are adrift in the blue,
Stately trees green beauty lend;
Orange lilies border golden fields,
Silvery mists bring rainbows near;
As magenta sunset glories fade
Soft, pale moonbeams will appear.

There's a symphony that greets the nose
As the summer breezes play;
Honeysuckle is wafted o'er
The fragrance of new-mown hay;
The exquisite perfume of the rose
Is distilled in dew and rain,
As the smell of harvest is muted
By sweet clover in the lane.

There's a symphony that greets the mind
As a summer day appears;
So play well your part in creation
In the music of the spheres.
Harmonize on a butterfly's wings,
Crescendo with ocean's roar,
Improvise on the tireless rhythms
That repeat forevermore.

Erma Stull Grove

Child, child,
Heart-free, foot-wild,
Hair, spun of gold in the sun,
Eyes flashing
Like raindrops splashing.
Child, sweet,
If you should meet someone
Whose eyes
Are searching the skies,
Bring him to earth
On your wings of mirth.
Dance for him, sing for him,
Let your voice ring for him,
He will remember that moment
Of rapture through years
That are long . . . Child, child,
Go with your song
Through sunshine and rain.
But child, child, remember
To pass here again.

Samuel Schierloh

You cannot teach a child to take care of himself unless you will let him try to take care of himself. He will make mistakes; and out of these mistakes will come his wisdom.

Henry Ward Beecher

The plays of naturally lively children are the infancy of art. Children live in a world of imagination and feeling. They invest the most insignificant object with any form they please, and see in it whatever they wish to see.

Adam G. Oehlenschlager

Staying Young

To be young, is not a matter of years. Youth lives forever in a love for the beauty that is in the world, in the mountains, the sea, the sky, and in lovely faces through which shines the kindliness of the inner mind.

It is the tuning into the orchestra of living sound, the soughing of the wind in the trees, the whisper and flow of the tide on wide beaches, the pounding of surf on the rocks, the chattering of brooks over the stones, the pattering of rain on leaves, the song of birds, and of peepers in the spring marshes, and the joyous lilt of sweet laughter.

Youth lives without counting the years in a fluid mind which is open to new theories, fresh opinions, changing impressions, and in the willingness to make new beginnings.

What is it to stay young? It is the ability to hold fast to old friends, and to make new ones, to keep forever our beloved in dear remembrance, and to open our hearts quickly to a light knock on the door.

Youth is to remain faithful to our beliefs, to preserve our enthusiasms, to trust in ourselves, to believe in our own courage, and to follow where courage bids us go.

And, at last, youth means that, like an unquestioning child, we place our hand without fear in the hand of the Gentle Guide, who will lead us through the little gate at the end of the winding road.

Cornelia Rogers

The faith to move mountains is the reward of those who have moved little hills.

Peace

I hear
the wind's soft whispers
in the night
like muted violins,
so soft and low
that chant a peaceful
upward flight
of thoughts, to still
life's restless
undertow.

I hear
the blue-green waters
running near
in calm and undulating
stream,
where grass and flowers,
bird and deer,
quaff peaceful draughts
of nature's
restful theme.

I hear
a million sounds
in evening's dusk
and see the myriad stars
blaze overhead,
while all about me,
scent of twilight musk
steals through my senses;
night and peace
are wed.

And I, who search
in nature's mystic dream,
find peace;
my soul joins
her symphonic theme.

Velta Myrle Allen

Not by Bread Alone

Man does not live by bread alone, but by beauty and harmony, truth and goodness, work and play, affection and friendship, aspiration and worship.

Man does not live by bread alone, but by the splendor of the starry firmament at midnight, the glory of the heavens at dawn, the gorgeous blending of colors at sunset, the luxurious loveliness of magnolia trees, the sheer magnificence of mountains.

Man does not live by bread alone, but by the majesty of ocean breakers, the shimmer of moonlight on a calm lake, the flashing silver of a mountain torrent, the exquisite patterns of snow crystals, the exalted creations of master-artists.

Man does not live by bread alone, but by the sweet song of a mockingbird, the rustle of tall corn in the breeze, the magic of the maestro's violin, the grandeur of Handel's *Messiah*, the sublimity of Beethoven's Fifth Symphony.

Man does not live by bread alone, but by the fragrance of roses, the scent of orange blossoms, the smell of new-mown hay, the clasp of a friend's hand, the tenderness of a mother's kiss.

Man does not live by bread alone, but by the lyrics and sonnets of poets, the mature wisdom of sages, the biographies of great souls, the life-giving works of Holy Scripture.

Man does not live by bread alone, but by comradeship and high adventure, seeking and finding, creating and cooperating, serving and sharing, loving and being loved.

Kirby Page

AUTUMN

Autumn is the time to work hard and choose a direction for the future. A person's individual reality is challenged, and undergoes many changes. The meaning and purpose of life is questioned and man searches for answers.

Jan F. Engel

Clairvoyant

The tree that lives a gypsy's life
Holds golden leaves within her fists;
Confetti-like she flings them out
As with the wind she waves her wrists.

The tree is always season-wise,
From truth she knows this magic thing.
The golden coins she spends today
Return all new to her next spring.

Peggy Windsor Garnett

Listen

Listen to the voice of a meadow calling,
Its fabric weaving rich mosaics
Round your ears
And beckoning to your buried soul
To follow.
Listen to the rain falling
On late autumn evenings
And the leaves rustling gently in the wind.
Then turn away,
Turn away to the glow of the fire
Of a wood hearth
With the sounds of their even breathing
Round your heart.

Janice Marianne Blue

Natural objects themselves, even when they make no claim to beauty, excite the feelings, and occupy the imagination. Nature pleases, attracts, delights, merely because it is nature. We recognize in it an infinite Power.

W. Humboldt

Worship

A forest at the dawning—
What a holy place to be
When all the sounds of morning
Swell into a symphony.

An anthem so majestic—
Rippling water, rustling leaves,
The waking call of nuthatch
Borne on a whisper-breeze.

My heart is turned to heaven
And my soul is tuned with God
In a mystic, sweet liaison
That transforms the earthy sod.

Fallen leaves become a carpet,
Misty sky, the vaulted arch;
The hillside is a pulpit;
Shaft of sun, the altar torch.

I think that no cathedral
Can hold the more of God
Than a forest at the dawning,
Breathing incense of the sod.

Marian C. Elliott

November Woods

Lovely are the silent woods
   in grey November days,
When the leaves fall red and gold
   about the quiet ways,
From massive beech, majestic oak
   and birches white and slim,
Like the pillared aisles of a cathedral
   vast and dim.

Drifting mist like smoking incense
   hangs upon the air . . .
Along the paths where birds once sang
   the trees stand stripped and bare,
Making Gothic arches
   with their branches interlaced,
And windows framing vistas,
   richly wrought and finely traced.

It is good to be in such a place
   on such a day . . .
Problems vanish from the mind
   and sorrows steal away;
In the woods of grey November
   silent and austere,
Nature gives her benediction
   to the passing year.

Patience Strong

From Out the Soil

Looking backward across the fields
As the sun drops in the west,
The farmer, tired but happy,
Turns toward home and needed rest.
First the faithful horses
Must be groomed with proper care,
Given refreshing drink and best of food.
For man, they did their share.

Tilling the ground and planting the seed,
Working from dawn until dark;
The creaking harness, the strain upon chain
To the song of the meadowlark.
The only sound that reaches his ear
As he plods through the heat of the day,
He feels the touch of the Hand of God
As he reverently bows to pray.

The life-giving seed, the fields well tilled,
He awaits and welcomes the showers;
He witnesses the miracle of creation,
In the warmth of the summer hours.
He sees fields of golden grain
Moving at the slightest breeze,
Reflecting the rays of the noonday sun,
Turning the whole into enchanted seas.

Contentedly he rests until the harvest moon
Calls him once again to the fields;
It is then he reaps a just reward
As he harvests what the good earth yields.
God expects us to do our part,
We cannot reap without toil,
But doing our share as man should do . . .
Great gifts come from out the soil.

R. H. Sotherland

The Touch of the Master's Hand

'Twas battered and scarred, and the auctioneer
Thought it scarcely worth his while
To waste much time on the old violin
But held it up with a smile.
"What am I bidden, good folks," he cried.
"Who'll start the bidding for me?"
"A dollar, a dollar"; then, "Two! Only two?
Two dollars, and who'll make it three?
Three dollars, once; three dollars, twice;
Going for three . . . " But no,
From the room, far back, a gray-haired man
Came forward and picked up the bow;
Then, wiping the dust from the old violin,
And tightening the loose strings,
He played a melody pure and sweet
As a caroling angel sings.

The music ceased, and the auctioneer,
With a voice that was quiet and low,
Said: "What am I bid for the old violin?"
And he held it up with the bow.
"A thousand dollars, and who'll make it two?
Two thousand! And who'll make it three?
Three thousand, once, three thousand, twice,
And going, and gone," said he.
The people cheered, but some of them cried,
"We do not quite understand
What changed its worth." Swift came the reply:
"The touch of a master's hand."

And many a man with life out of tune,
And battered and scarred with sin,
Is auctioned cheap to the thoughtless crowd,
Much like the old violin.
A "mess of pottage," a glass of wine;
A game— and he travels on.
He is "going" once, and "going" twice,
He's "going" and almost "gone."
But the Master comes, and the foolish crowd
Never can quite understand
The worth of a soul and the change that's wrought
By the touch of the Master's hand.

Myra Brooks Welch

On Work

Life is indeed darkness save when there
is urge,
And all urge is blind save when there
is knowledge,
And all knowledge is vain save when
there is work,
And all work is empty save when there
is love;
And when you work with love you
bind yourself to yourself, and to one
another, and to God.
And what is it to work with love?
It is to weave the cloth with threads
drawn from your heart, even as if
your beloved were to wear that cloth.
It is to build a house with affection,
even as if your beloved were to dwell
in that house.
It is to sow seeds with tenderness and
reap the harvest with joy, even as if
your beloved were to eat the fruit.
It is to charge all things you fashion
with a breath of your own spirit.

Kahlil Gibran

I like autumn best of all, because its
leaves are a little yellow, its tone mel-
lower, its colors richer, and it is tinged a
little with sorrow. Its golden richness speaks
not of the innocence of spring, nor of the
power of summer, but of the mellowness
and kindly wisdom of approaching age.
It knows the limitations of life and is
content.

Lin Yutang

Song of the Wheat

The wind's deft fingers pluck the golden strings,
And music runs like light along the wheat:
Laughter is there and a bright gladness sings
An ancient song of fields that are replete
In their fulfilment where each golden head
Is rife with the precious essences of bread.

It is the song of wheat, a song of praise
For sun and moon and stars and clear cool rain,
For the heady ecstasy of summer days,
For long dark nights and perfect growing grain,
And for the earnest labor that distills
Those essences in far-off shining mills.

A song of future loaves, well-baked, to feed
A hungry world in its stark, desperate need.

Grace Noll Crowell

Interlude

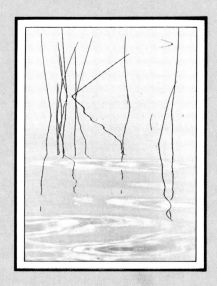

A mellowed radiance is here
As autumn gleams through misty haze,
And all the color of the year
Burns slowly out in smoky blaze.
This interlude of tranquil charm
Before the blanketing of snow
Transforms the countryside and farm
With this subdued, bronze-tinted glow.

The sepia leaves upon the ground
Beneath the feet of squirrel and hare
Give forth a papery, rustling sound
Upon the mild October air,
And nuts fall softly day and night.
Now streams flow leisurely along,
And overhead in southward flight
A late bird spins a good-bye song.

Donalda von Poellnitz

Results

There is more to a life than merely the living;
    The end of a journey counts more than the start;
There is less to be had from getting than giving,
    And more to a master than lessons in art.

There's more to a game than merely the playing—
    There's less in the winning than effort involved;
The making of debts is less hard than the paying;
    There's more to a question than "Be it resolved."

There is more in belief than merely believing,
    For faith fosters action and action bears fruit;
There's more in a lie than the act of deceiving—
    The same seed that sprouted grows also a root.

The difference is slight at the point of dividing
    Between good and evil, but what of the goal?
Look well to the end of the road when deciding
    The eternal trend of the quest of the soul.

Myra Brooks Welch

Who sees the wonders of a foggy day
And understands the blessings of its worth
Will pause to look on life with quiet eyes
And hear the subtle heartbeat of the earth.

Rena Przychocki

Hands

I do not ask for sculptured ivory hands
Whose lily whiteness softens to the touch—
Though beauty, for itself, is much desired.
The beauty I desire is not so much
Of scented lily cups. My hands will know
The moist warm feel of loamy furrowed earth—
And more, the hard round handle of the hoe.

But make them soft enough to dry the cheeks
Where little tears are spilled; and skilled to mend
Where overalls, and hearts, and lives are torn.
And on occasion, strengthen them to lend
An ivory firmness, when the cause is right.
But oh, toward the ending of the day,
Give them the suppleness to fold and pray.

Ora Pate Stewart

Hands

Hands are the bread of the toiler,
A mother's soft caress,
The creative skill of the craftsman's will
And all that dreams express.

Hands are the outstretched token
Of friendship's noble art,
The sturdy grasp and assuring clasp
Of the true and trusting heart.

Hands are the health and healing
Of mercy's white domain,
The surgeon's art, the nurse's part,
The pity for the pain.

Hands are prayer's devotion
Twined in a fleshly scroll,
Postured fingers where reverence lingers,
The language of the soul.

The hourglass still is flowing,
The path is yet untrod,
O days to be! Help me to see
That hands are the tools of God!

Alfred Grant Walton

I have been driven many times to my knees
By the overwhelming conviction
That I had nowhere else to go.
My own wisdom, and that of all about me,
Seemed insufficient for the day.

Abraham Lincoln

Prayer of St. Francis

Lord, make me an instrument of
   Thy peace.
Where there is hatred, let me
   sow love;
Where there is injury, pardon;
Where there is doubt, faith;
When there is despair, hope;
Where there is darkness, light;
When there is sadness, joy.

O Divine Master, grant that
I may not so much seek
To be consoled, as to console;
Not so much to be understood as
To understand; not so much to be
Loved as to love:
For it is in giving that
   we receive;
It is in pardoning, that we
   are pardoned;
It is in dying, that we awaken
   to eternal life.

St. Francis of Assisi

If

If you can keep your head when all about you
　　Are losing theirs and blaming it on you,
If you can trust yourself when all men doubt you,
　　But make allowance for their doubting too;
If you can wait and not be tired by waiting,
　　Or being lied about, don't deal in lies,
Or being hated, don't give way to hating,
　　And yet don't look too good, nor talk too wise:

If you can dream—and not make dreams your master;
　　If you can think—and not make thoughts your aim;
If you can meet with Triumph and Disaster
　　And treat those two impostors just the same;
If you can bear to hear the truth you've spoken
　　Twisted by knaves to make a trap for fools,
Or watch the things you gave your life to, broken,
　　And stoop and build 'em up with worn-out tools:

If you can make one heap of all your winnings
　　And risk it on one turn of pitch-and-toss,
And lose, and start again at your beginnings
　　And never breathe a word about your loss;
If you can force your heart and nerve and sinew
　　To serve your turn long after they are gone,
And so hold on when there is nothing in you
　　Except the Will which says to them: "Hold on!"

If you can talk with crowds and keep your virtue,
　　Or walk with Kings—nor lose the common touch,
If neither foes nor loving friends can hurt you,
　　If all men count with you, but none too much;
If you can fill the unforgiving minute
　　With sixty seconds' worth of distance run,
Yours is the Earth and everything that's in it,
　　And—which is more—you'll be a Man, my son!

　　　　　　　　　　　　　　　　Rudyard Kipling

Autumn

Autumn is the time for remembering summer's gentle breezes . . . the time for crisp bright-colored leaves to fall to the earth below. All summer long they have hung overhead in lacy formation, their life-span one short spring and summer, making room for the new buds to rest during the winter . . . to bring forth new life in the spring . . . Fall is a bright and glorious end to their short stay.

Autumn is the time for strolling through flaming country lanes . . . the time for discovering the beauty that lies within our grasp, the crisp fall breezes, the bright blue skies, the fiery-colored trees, their leaves shimmering in the sun like so many golden coins, the rustle of leaves underfoot, the hint of the frost to come hanging in the air.

Autumn is the time for the readying of winter's icy breath, the time for woolly sweaters and softly-glowing fireplaces . . . a time for crunchy apples and freshly popped corn, a time for good smells from the kitchen, a time for the gathering of friends before the fireplace, a time for a drive through the woods, not too long ago, green and bursting with life . . . now a wonderland of colors to delight the eye and gladden the heart.

Autumn is the time for the city to gather its wandering children after their summer of excursions here and there . . . to call them from abroad, to promise them the best she has to offer . . . the brilliant opening of song, music and dance, the store windows all dressed for cooler weather, a breeze rolling in off the river not quite cool enough to let you forget the summer.

Carol A. Davis

Country Storekeeper

The keeper of the country store has
    a most enchanting place
That smells of coffee, cheese and
    spices; and with an easy grace
He measures yards of calico, puts up
    beans or fish,
Penny candy, magic yeast,
    most anything you wish.

He visits with his neighbors and
    knows everyone by name;
At times, by the potbellied stove,
    he'll play a checker game.
The cracker barrel is standing near,
    fresh eggs and butter, too,
Maple sugar; and he'll spin a
    country tale or two.

Not only can we find in here real
    treasures on the shelves;
But in this homey atmosphere, we
    garner for ourselves
Bits of wisdom, laughter, peace,
    which folks need more and more,
And it doesn't even cost a cent
    in the country store.

Ruth B. Field

INTER

Winter's tranquil tone reflects a person' inner self at this time of year. As the snow sleeps on the earth in quiet repose, so do a person's dreams touch the heart, creating an introspective search for identity. A quiescent mood allows a person to view the motion of things around him, and believe in things that hold new promises

Jan F. Enge

The Silent Winter

And now come the silent days of inward living . . . the profitable hours of meditative peace. Without, white fields are full of snowy silences; within, the welcome warmth of hearth and home, the open book, where march great thoughts to lead us far afield through legend, song and story. Now, if ever, should our summer dreams come true . . . our hearts attain their aspirations . . . our hands fulfill their long-awaited duties; now should our faith renew its hold on God and truth and our very souls climb upward to their heaven. For lo! the silent winter is the spirit's spring.

Edwin Osgood Grover

A Time to Meditate

The heart must have its wintertime,
A time to meditate, when peace,
Like snow, descends with calming grace
And all the fruitless worries cease.

The heart must have its wintertime,
A time when dreams, like roots, can sleep
And gather strength until the day
They have a rendezvous to keep.

The heart must have its wintertime,
An interlude when hope sprouts wings
As bright as any cardinal's,
And newborn courage softly sings.

The heart must have its time of snow
To rest in silence and to grow.

Marie Daerr Boehringer

You are richer today than you were yesterday if you have laughed often, given something, forgiven even more, made a new friend today, or made stepping-stones of stumbling blocks. If you have thought more in terms of "thyself" than "myself," or if you have managed to be cheerful even though you were weary. You are richer tonight than you were this morning if you have taken time to trace the handiwork of God in the commonplace things of life, or if you have learned to count out things which really do not count, or if you have been a little blinder to the faults of friend and foe. You are far richer if a little child has smiled at you, and a stray dog has licked your hand, or if you have looked for the best in others and given others the best in you.

Author Unknown

Wonder

Wonder is the intangible, elusive,
Breathtaking miracle
Found in the commonplace.
It lives in the symmetry of snowflakes,
The symphony of trees at dawn,
The splendor of a snow-swept day.
Quietly it may appear
In the understanding of sorrow,
The bright beauty of a promise,
A tender word spoken.
Children are one with it;
Hearts which hold love
Recognize and cherish it.
Birth and death
Are imbued with its touch.
To lose it is to be ever apart
From dreams and hope and joy.
To share it is to live forever.

Doris Chalma Brock

Nature is beautiful, always beautiful! Every little flake of snow is a perfect crystal; and they fall together as gracefully as if fairies of the air caught waterdrops and made them into artificial flowers to garland the wings of the wind!

Lydia M. Child

I Love Antiques

I love antiques because
They have so much to say
Of life in other years,
Of another time, another day.
They're old and worn; but beauty
Lies hidden deep inside,
And were to someone, one time,
A possession of great pride.
An old clock marking hours,
A lantern lighting bygone days,
A lamp with roses on it
Still sheds its soft-like rays.

I love antiques, where ghosts
From long ago will not depart.
The echo of a child still sings
To a doll with a sawdust heart.
The sweetest of them all to me
Is the rocker that has known
The love of child and mother
That once made a house a home.
An old rosewood piano
Awaits with silent keys
But only hears the music
Of the wind through ancient trees.

I love antiques that tell
Of a bygone simple life,
With old-time things
Loved by some cheerful wife:
An iron cookstove,
Once warm and bright,
A tall bedstead way upstairs,
So cold on a winter night;
An ancient wooden rocking horse
Some little boy loved so
Still holds his youthful fingerprints
Pressed there long ago.

Lucille Crumley

Ethereal Beauty

There's a world outside my window,
Far removed from all around,
Where I feel a transformation
As a soul when peace is found.

Through the velvet settling darkness
Of the wintry night
Glows the iridescent beauty
Of the city light.
Just enough to create magic,
Making shadows everywhere,
While the sparkling snowflakes glisten
As a blanket lying there;
And the wind in soft caresses
Gently sighs through mourning pines,
In a world of melancholy
With a spirit kin to mine.

Or the mood can be so different
On a misty, rainy night
When just dimly through the vapors
Threads the golden touch of light.
So intriguing in the stillness
Is the mood of world a-borning
That I feel this must be Eden
On that distant glorious morning.

And I think that surely angels
Must come here in glad surprise
When they find such perfect beauty
Far away from heaven's skies,
For on balmy summer evenings
Stars bejewel the azure dome
And the light streams through the branches
Of the sentinels of home,
Bathing everything in gold dust
From the dewy green below
To the topmost of the needles
Where the breezes whisper low;
And the lacy shadows falling
From the master Artist's hand
Clothe the gentle slopes and valleys
In the garb of wonderland.

As a hesitating mortal,
Undeserving of so much,
I behold ethereal beauty
That has felt the Maker's touch.

Betty Burton Choate

Reflections of Home

When winter's blanket wraps around the old familiar home, and daylight's call is shortened as the darkness comes to roam, what pleasure then to notice, as the evening hours appear, that the heirloom lamps are glowing, shedding light so warm and clear.

The well-worn path seems trim and bright as it leads to the old oak porch, where from a blackened hook had hung a lantern as a torch to guide all who would enter, at whatever hour of time, with a friendly cheery greeting that the heart found quite sublime.

The moonlight playing hide and seek across the weathered frame gave thought that maybe, just by chance, could all this be the same?

Though winter's chill will pass away, the home remains in a heart where roots are firmly planted in a spiritual counterpart.

Olive Dunkelberger

Something Lovely

Let me find something lovely when I wake . . .
Not a rich garment that I may put on,
Or something valued for the value's sake,
But something lovely when these things
   are gone:

Perhaps a whistle by a passing boy,
Perhaps a letter from an absent friend,
Something to fill my little cup of joy
   until day's end.

Let me bring something lovely when I come . . .
No matter where, no matter whose the door,
Not something lovely that is valued more:
Perhaps a smile, perhaps a word of cheer,
Perhaps a high resolve my best to do,
Something to last when even night is near
   and day is through.

Let me leave something lovely when I go . . .
Not something that I jostled men to win,
Not something valued for the value so,
But for some loveliness that lies within:
Perhaps a garden or perhaps a book,
Perhaps a gentle daughter, manly son;
For then how lovely even night will look
   when day is done.

Douglas Malloch

Goals are like stars;
They may not be reached
But they can always
Be a guide.

Author Unknown

Men and Stars

To go into solitude, a man needs to retire as much from his chamber as from society. I am not solitary whilst I read and write, though nobody is with me. But if a man would be alone, let him look at the stars. The rays that come from heavenly worlds will separate between him and what he touches. One might think the atmosphere was made transparent with this design, to give man, in the heavenly bodies, the perpetual presence of the sublime. Seen in the streets of cities, how great they are! If the stars should appear one night in a thousand years, how would men believe and adore, and preserve for many generations the remembrance of the city of God which had been shown! But every night come out these envoys of beauty, and light the universe with their admonishing smile.

Henry Ward Beecher

As the moon and the stars hide in the glare of the day, so does the light of our inner selves; unfolding to us in the unhurried pace of the night.

Jan F. Engel

A Candle in the Night

So very many people
Are like a candle in the night.
Their gentle noiseless beauty
Is like a steady burning light.

Though they be short and tiny
Or shapely tapers tall and fair,
Around them beams a radiance
That brightens life and steals our care.

They do not sense the darkness
Because their self-effacing glow
Encircles them with beauty
That shines alike on friend or foe.

And so I watch the candles
That banish darkness in the night,
Though they be short and tiny
Or tapers tall with flames of light.

Mary Stoner Wine

Old and Young

All love is beauty
Regardless of time;
Old love is music,
Young love is rhyme.
Old love is depth,
And young love is height;
Old love is warmth,
And young love is light.
Old love is bondage,
Tempered and mild;
Young love is freedom,
Windblown and wild.
Old love is pleasure;
Young love is thrill!
Old love is reason;
Young love is will.
Old love is certain
As summer and fall;
Young, has no limits;
Young love is all!
Old love has wisdom
From memory's shelf;
Old love knows volumes,
Young, but itself!
Old love is seasoned,
Has weathered its test;
Yet tender, untried,
Young love is best!

Frank H. Keith

Age of Inquiry . . .

I'd have to be a Socrates,
At least a Solomon,
To answer all the questions
Posed by one grandson.
I explain in simple language,
I measure each reply,
I tell him everything I know;
And still he asks me, "Why?"

Helen Virden

Smile

A smile costs nothing but gives much. It enriches those who receive, without making poorer those who give. It takes but a moment, but the memory of it sometimes lasts forever. None is so rich or mighty that he gets along without it and none is so poor but that he can be made rich by it. A smile creates happiness in the home, fosters goodwill in business and is the countersign of friendship. It brings rest to the weary, cheer to the discouraged, sunshine to the sad, and is nature's best antidote for trouble. Yet it cannot be bought, begged, borrowed or stolen for it is something that is of no value to anyone until it is given away. Some people are too tired to give you a smile; give them one of yours, as none needs a smile so much as he who has no more to give.

Author Unknown

Silence

I paused to listen to the silence. My breath crystallized as it passed my cheeks, drifted on a breeze gentler than a whisper. The wind vane pointed toward the South Pole. Presently the wind cups ceased their gentle turning as the cold killed the breeze. My frozen breath hung like a cloud overhead.

The day was dying, the night was being born— but with great peace. Here were the imponderable processes and forces of the cosmos, harmonious and soundless. Harmony, that was it! That was what came out of the silence— a gentle rhythm, the strain of a perfect chord, the music of the spheres, perhaps.

It was enough to catch that rhythm, momentarily to be myself a part of it. In that instant I could feel no doubt of man's oneness with universe. The conviction came that that rhythm was too orderly, too harmonious, too perfect to be a product of blind chance— that, therefore, there must be purpose in the whole and that man was part of that whole and not an accidental offshoot. It was a feeling that transcended reason, that went to the heart of man's despair and found it groundless. The universe was a cosmos, not a chaos; man was as rightfully a part of that cosmos as were the day and night.

Richard E. Byrd

Reprinted by permission of G.P. Putnam's Sons from ALONE by Admiral Richard E. Byrd. Copyright 1938 by Richard E. Byrd. Copyright renewed © 1966 by Marie E. Byrd.

The Weaver

I sat by my loom in silence,
Facing the western sky.
The warp was rough and tangled;
The threads did unevenly fly.
Impatient, I pulled at the fibers;
They snapped and flew from my hands.
Weary and faint and sore hearted,
I gathered the broken strands.

I had beautiful colors to work with—
White, blue like the heavens above—
And tangled in all the meshes
Were the golden threads of love;
But the colors were dulled by my handling,
The pattern was faded and gray,
That once to my eager seeming
Shone fairer than flowers of May.

But, alas, not the half of my pattern
Was finished at set of sun;
What should I say to the Master
When I hear him call, "Is it done?"
I threw down my shuttle in sorrow
(I had worked through the livelong day)
And I lay down to slumber in darkness,
Too weary even to pray.

In my dreams a vision of splendor,
An angel, smiling faced,
With gentle and tender finger
The work of the weavers traced.
He stooped with a benediction
O'er the loom of my neighbor near,
For the threads were smooth and even
And the pattern perfect and clear.

Then I waited in fear and trembling,
As he stood by my tangled skein,
For the look of reproach and pity
That I knew would add to my pain.
Instead, with a thoughtful aspect,
He turned his gaze upon me;
And I knew that he saw the fair picture
Of my work as I hoped it would be.

And with touch divine of his finger,
He traced my faint copy anew,
Transforming the clouded colors
And letting the pattern shine true;
And I knew in that moment of waiting,
While His look pierced my very soul through,
I was judged not so much by my doing
As by what I had striven to do.

Author Unknown

The Spinner

Now Time is endlessly spinning,
  Meting out moments each day.
And each man gets his own portion
  To use in his self-chosen way.

For some, the time is sufficient;
  Life is a sweet sounding bell.
The chaff has been lost in the spinning
  And pathways are brightened as well.

Some give us words of true wisdom
  That fall as the deep-winter snow:
With visions of beauty to ponder,
  Enriching wherever they go.

A few find the secret of living:
  This moment is all that there is.
Since God works His wonders in moments,
  How precious the treasure Time gives!

Alice Leedy Mason

Believe in the World

I believe in the world and its bigness and splendor;
That most of the hearts beating round us are tender;
That days are but footsteps and years are but miles
That lead us to beauty and singing and smiles;
That roses that blossom and toilers that plod
Are filled with the glorious spirit of God.

I believe in the purpose of everything living;
That taking is but the forerunner of giving;
That strangers are friends that we some day may meet;
And not all the bitter can equal the sweet;
That creeds are but colors, and no man has said
That God loves the yellow rose more than the red.

I believe in the path that today I am treading;
That I shall come safe through the dangers I'm dreading;
That even the scoffer shall turn from his ways
And some day be won back to trust and to praise;
That the leaf on the tree and the thing we call man
Are sharing alike in His infinite plan.

I believe that all things that are living and breathing
Some richness of beauty to earth are bequeathing;
That all that goes out of this world leaves behind
Some duty accomplished for mortals to find;
That the humblest of creatures our praise is deserving;
For it, with the wisest, the Master is serving.

Edgar A. Guest

Copyrighted 1932. Used by permission of Reilly & Lee Co.

designed by
Jan Frances Engel

Editorial Director, James Kuse
Managing Editor, Ralph Luedtke
Photographic Editor, Gerald Koser
Production Editor, Stuart L. Zyduck

ACKNOWLEDGMENTS

CAMPING by Larry Roger Clark. From SPEAK TO THE EARTH by Larry Roger Clark. Copyright © 1972 by Larry Roger Clark. Published by Dorrance & Company. SYMPHONY OF SUMMER by Erma Stull Grove. From THE FOOTPRINT OF GOD by Erma Stull Grove. Copyright © 1969 by Erma Stull Grove. Published by Dorrance & Company. FRIENDSHIP HOUSE by James J. Metcalfe. Copyrighted. Courtesy Field Enterprises, Inc. TO A FRIEND by Lorice Fiani Mulhern. From REALMS OF ENCHANTMENT by Lorice Fiani Mulhern. Copyright © 1970 by Lorice Fiani Mulhern. Published by Dorrance & Company. Our sincere thanks to the following authors whose addresses we were unable to locate: Maurine Hathaway for MY HAPPY SONG SHALL ECHO . . . and Cornelia Rogers for STAYING YOUNG.